Logans ; bk. 3

Praise for
SONG OF THE TREES

"A triumphant book . . . A true story truly told."
—*The New York Times*

"Brings to light the incredible fight for respect and honor still facing black families in the United States in the twentieth century."
—*Children's Literature*

"A moving story that manifests two simple, strongly felt emotions: a love of nature and a sense of self-respect."
—*Booklist*

"The simple story has been written with great conviction and strength, and Cassie's descriptions of the trees add a poetic touch."
—*The Horn Book*

WINNER OF THE COUNCIL ON INTERRACIAL BOOKS AWARD

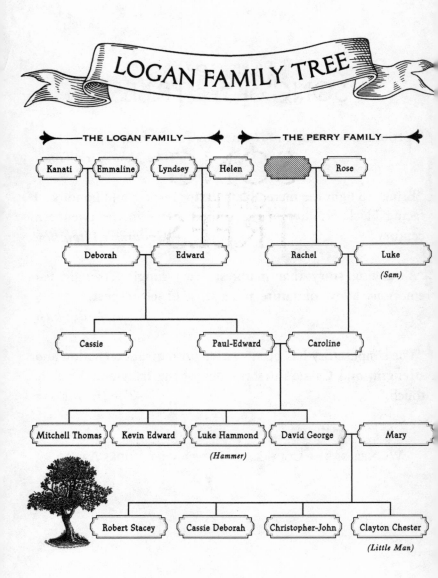

LOGAN FAMILY TREE

THE LOGAN FAMILY ——— THE PERRY FAMILY

Kanati — Emmaline   Lyndsey — Helen   ▨ — Rose

Deborah   Edward   Rachel — Luke *(Sam)*

Cassie   Paul-Edward — Caroline

Mitchell Thomas   Kevin Edward   Luke Hammond *(Hammer)*   David George — Mary

Robert Stacey   Cassie Deborah   Christopher-John   Clayton Chester *(Little Man)*

SONG
OF THE
TREES

MILDRED D. TAYLOR

SONG
OF THE
TREES

PICTURES BY JERRY PINKNEY

PUFFIN BOOKS

PUFFIN BOOKS
An imprint of Penguin Random House LLC
375 Hudson Street
New York, New York 10014

First published in the United States of America
by Dial Books for Young Readers,
a division of Penguin Putnam Books for Young Readers, 1975
Published by Puffin Books,
a division of Penguin Putnam Books for Young Readers, 2003
This edition published by Puffin Books,
an imprint of Penguin Random House LLC, 2016

THE LIBRARY OF CONGRESS HAS CATALOGED THE DIAL BOOKS EDITION AS FOLLOWS:
Taylor, Mildred D., Song of the trees.
[1. Trees—Fiction. 2. Depressions—1929—Fiction.]
I. Pinkney, Jerry, ill.   II. Title.
PZ7.T21723So [Fic]   74-18598
ISBN: 0-8037-5452-3 (hardcover) ISBN: 0-8037-5453-1 (lib. bdg.)

Puffin Books ISBN 978-0-14-250075-0

Book design by Cara Petrus

Printed in the United States of America

27 29 30 28

This book is dedicated:

To my mother, Mrs. Deletha M. Taylor, the quiet, lovely one, who urged perseverance;

To my father, Mr. Wilbert L. Taylor, the strong, steadfast one, who wove the tales of history;

To my sister, Miss Wilma M. Taylor, the beautiful, laughing one, who lifted my spirits high;

and

To my grandparents, Mrs. Lee Annie Bryant, Mr. Hugh Taylor, and Mrs. Lou Emma Taylor, the wise ones, who bridged the generations between slavery and freedom;

and

To the Family, who fought and survived.

This book is based on a true story, one that actually happened in my family. As a small child, I often listened to my father recount his adventures growing up in rural Mississippi during the Depression. His vivid description of the giant trees, the coming of the lumbermen, and the events that followed made me feel that I too was present. I hope my readers will be as moved by the story as I was.

Mildred D. Taylor
October 1974

"Cassie. Cassie, child, wake up now," Big Ma called gently as the new sun peeked over the horizon.

I looked sleepily at my grandmother and closed my eyes again.

"Cassie! Get up, girl!" This time the voice was not so gentle.

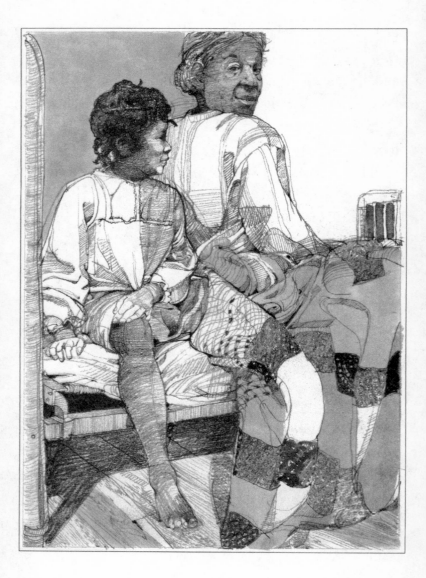

I jumped out of the deep feathery bed as Big Ma climbed from the other side. The room was still dark, and I stubbed my toe while stumbling sleepily about looking for my clothes.

"Shoot! Darn ole chair," I fussed, rubbing my injured foot.

"Hush, Cassie, and open them curtains if you can't see," Big Ma said. "Prop that window open, too, and let some of that fresh morning air in here."

I opened the window and looked outside. The earth was draped in a cloak of gray mist as the sun chased the night away. The cotton stalks, which in another hour would glisten greenly toward the sun, were gray. The ripening corn, wrapped in jackets of emerald and gold, was gray. Even the rich brown Mississippi earth was gray.

Only the trees of the forest were not gray. They stood dark, almost black, across the dusty road, still holding the night. A soft breeze stirred, and their voices whispered down to me in a song of morning greeting.

"Cassie, girl, I said open that window, not stand there gazing out all morning. Now, get moving before I take something to you," Big Ma threatened.

I dashed to my clothes. Before Big Ma had unwoven her long braid of gray hair, my pants and shirt were on and I was hurrying into the kitchen.

A small kerosine lamp was burning in a corner as I entered. Its light reflected on seven-year-old Christopher-John, short, pudgy and a year younger than me, sitting sleepily upon a side bench drinking a large glass of clabber milk. Mama's back was to me. She was dipping flour from a near-empty canister, while my older brother, Stacey, built a fire in the huge iron-bellied stove.

"I don't know what I'm going to do with you, Christopher-John," Mama scolded. "Getting up in the middle of the night and eating all that cornbread. Didn't you have enough to eat before you went to bed?"

"Yes'm," Christopher-John murmured.

"Lord knows I don't want any of my babies going hungry, but times are hard, honey. Don't you know folks all around here in Mississippi are struggling? Children crying cause they got no food to eat, and their daddies crying cause they can't get jobs so they can feed their babies? And you getting up in the middle of the night, stuffing yourself with cornbread!"

Her voice softened as she looked at the sleepy little boy. "Baby, we're in a depression. Why do you think Papa's way down in Louisiana laying tracks on the railroad? So his children can eat—but only when they're hungry. You understand?"

"Yes'm," Christopher-John murmured again as his eyes slid blissfully shut.

"Morning, Mama," I chimed.

"Morning, baby," Mama said. "You wash up yet?"

"No'm."

"Then go wash up and call Little Man again. Tell him he's not dressing to meet President Roosevelt this morning. Hurry up now cause I want you to set the table."

Little Man, a very small six-year-old and a most finicky dresser, was brushing his hair when I entered the room he shared with Stacey and Christopher-John. His blue pants were faded, but except for a small grass stain on one knee, they were clean. Outside of his Sunday pants, these were the only pants he had, and he was always careful to keep them in the best condition possible. But one look at him and I knew that he was far from pleased with their condition this morning. He frowned down at the spot for a moment, then continued brushing.

"Man, hurry up and get dressed," I called. "Mama said you ain't dressing to meet the president."

"See there," he said, pointing at the stain. "You did that."

"I did no such thing. You fell all by yourself."

"You tripped me!"

"Didn't!"

"Did, too!"

"Hey, cut it out, you two!" ordered Stacey, entering the room. "You fought over that stupid stain yesterday. Now get moving, both of you. We gotta go pick blackberries before the sun gets too high. Little Man, you go gather the eggs while Christopher-John and me milk the cows."

Little Man and I decided to settle our dispute later when Stacey wasn't around. With Papa away, eleven-year-old Stacey thought of himself as the man of the house, and Mama had instructed Little Man, Christopher-John, and me to mind him. So, like it or not, we humored him. Besides, he was bigger than we were.

I ran to the back porch to wash. When I returned to the kitchen, Mama was talking to Big Ma.

"We got about enough flour for two more meals,"

Mama said, cutting the biscuit dough. "Our salt and sugar are practically down to nothing and ——" She stopped when she saw me. "Cassie, baby, go gather the eggs for Mama."

"Little Man's gathering the eggs."

"Then go help him."

"But I ain't set the table yet."

"Set it when you come back."

I knew that I was not wanted in the kitchen. I looked suspiciously at my mother and grandmother, then went to the back porch to get a basket.

Big Ma's voice drifted through the open window. "Mary, you oughta write David and tell him somebody done opened his letter and stole that ten dollars he sent," she said.

"No, Mama. David's got enough on his mind. Besides, there's enough garden foods so we won't go hungry."

"But what 'bout your medicine? You're all out of it and the doctor told you good to ——"

"Shhhh!" Mama stared at the window. "Cassie, I thought I told you to go gather those eggs!"

"I had to get a basket, Mama!" I hurried off the porch and ran to the barn.

After breakfast when the sun was streaking red across the sky, my brothers and I ambled into the coolness of the forest leading our three cows and their calves down the narrow cow path to the pond. The morning was already muggy, but the trees closed out the heat as their leaves waved restlessly, high above our heads.

"Good morning, Mr. Trees," I shouted. They answered me with a soft, swooshing sound. "Hear 'em, Stacey? Hear 'em singing?"

"Ah, cut that out, Cassie. Them trees ain't singing. How many times I gotta tell you that's just the wind?" He stopped at a sweet alligator gum, pulled out his knife and scraped off a glob of gum that had seeped through its cracked bark. He handed me half.

As I stuffed the gooey wad into my mouth, I patted the tree and whispered, "Thank you, Mr. Gum Tree."

Stacey frowned at me, then looked back at Christopher-John and Little Man walking far behind us, munching on their breakfast biscuits.

"Man! Christopher-John! Come on, now," he yelled. "If we finish the berry picking early, we can go wading before we go back."

Christopher-John and Little Man ran to catch up with

us. Then, resuming their leisurely pace, they soon fell behind again.

A large gray squirrel scurried across our path and up a walnut tree. I watched until it was settled amidst the tree's featherlike leaves; then, poking one of the calves, I said, "Stacey, is Mama sick?"

"Sick? Why you say that?"

"Cause I heard Big Ma asking her 'bout some medicine she's supposed to have."

Stacey stopped, a worried look on his face. "If she's sick, she ain't bad sick," he decided. "If she was bad sick, she'd been in bed."

We left the cows at the pond and, taking our berry baskets, delved deeper into the forest looking for the wild blackberry bushes.

"I see one!" I shouted.

"Where?" cried Christopher-John, eager for the sweet berries.

"Over there! Last one to it's a rotten egg!" I yelled, and off I ran.

Stacey and Little Man followed at my heels. But Christopher-John puffed far behind. "Hey, wait for me," he cried.

"Let's hide from Christopher-John," Stacey suggested.

The three of us ran in different directions. I plunged behind a giant old pine and hugged its warm trunk as I waited for Christopher-John.

Christopher-John puffed to a stop; then, looking all around, called, "Hey, Stacey! Cassie! Hey, Man! Y'all cut that out!"

I giggled and Christopher-John heard me.

"I see you, Cassie!" he shouted, starting toward me as fast as his chubby legs would carry him. "You're it!"

"Not 'til you tag me," I laughed. As I waited for him to get closer, I glanced up into the boughs of my wintry-smelling hiding tree expecting a song of laughter. But the old pine only tapped me gently with one of its long, low branches. I turned from the tree and dashed away.

"You can't, you can't, you can't catch me," I taunted, dodging from one beloved tree to the next. Around shaggy-bark hickories and sharp-needled pines, past blue-gray beeches and sturdy black walnuts I sailed while my laughter resounded through the ancient forest, filling every chink. Overhead, the boughs of the giant trees hovered protectively, but they did not join in my laughter.

Deeper into the forest I plunged.

Christopher-John, unable to keep up, plopped on the ground in a pant. Little Man and Stacey, emerging from their hiding places, ran up to him.

"Ain't you caught her yet?" Little Man demanded, more than a little annoyed.

"He can't catch the champ," I boasted, stopping to rest against a hickory tree. I slid my back down the tree's shaggy trunk and looked up at its long branches, heavy with sweet nuts and slender green leaves, perfectly still. I looked around at the leaves of the other trees. They were still also. I stared at the trees, aware of an eerie silence descending over the forest.

Stacey walked toward me. "What's the matter with you, Cassie?" he asked.

"The trees, Stacey," I said softly, "they ain't singing no more."

"Is that all?" He looked up at the sky. "Come on, y'all. It's getting late. We'd better go pick them berries." He turned and walked on.

"But, Stacey, listen. Little Man, Christopher-John, listen."

The forest echoed an uneasy silence.

"The wind just stopped blowing, that's all," said Stacey. "Now stop fooling around and come on."

I jumped up to follow Stacey, then cried, "Stacey, look!" On a black oak a few yards away was a huge white X. "How did that get there?" I exclaimed, running to the tree.

"There's another one!" Little Man screamed.

"I see one too!" shouted Christopher-John.

Stacey said nothing as Christopher-John, Little Man and I ran wildly through the forest counting the ghost-like marks.

"Stacey, they're on practically all of them," I said when he called us back. "Why?"

Stacey studied the trees, then suddenly pushed us down.

"My clothes!" Little Man wailed indignantly.

"Hush, Man, and stay down," Stacey warned. "Somebody's coming."

Two white men emerged. We looked at each other. We knew to be silent.

"You mark them all down here?" one of the men asked.

"Not the younger ones, Mr. Andersen."

"We might need them, too," said Mr. Andersen, count-

ing the X's. "But don't worry 'bout marking them now, Tom. We'll get them later. Also them trees up past the pond toward the house."

"The old woman agree to you cutting these trees?"

"I ain't been down there yet," Mr. Andersen said.

"Mr. Andersen . . ." Tom hesitated a moment, looked up at the silent trees, then back at Mr. Andersen. "Maybe you should go easy with them," he cautioned. "You know that David can be as mean as an ole jackass when he wanna be."

"He's talking about Papa," I whispered.

"Shhhh!" Stacey hissed.

Mr. Andersen looked uneasy. "What's that gotta do with anything?"

"Well, he just don't take much to any dealings with white folks." Again, Tom looked up at the trees. "He ain't afraid like some."

Mr. Andersen laughed weakly. "Don't worry 'bout that, Tom. The land belongs to his mama. He don't have no say in it. Besides, I guess I oughta know how to handle David Logan. After all, there are ways. . . .

"Now, you get on back to my place and get some boys and start chopping down these trees," Mr. Andersen said.

"I'll go talk to the old woman." He looked up at the sky. "We can almost get a full day's work in if we hurry."

Mr. Andersen turned to walk away, but Tom stopped him. "Mr. Andersen, you really gonna chop all the trees?"

"If I need to. These folks ain't got no call for them. I do. I got me a good contract for these trees and I aim to fulfill it."

Tom watched Mr. Andersen walk away; then, looking sorrowfully up at the trees, he shook his head and disappeared into the depths of the forest.

"What we gonna do, Stacey?" I asked anxiously. "They can't just cut down our trees, can they?"

"I don't know. Papa's gone . . ." Stacey muttered to himself, trying to decide what we should do next.

"Boy, if Papa was here, them ole white men wouldn't be messing with our trees," Little Man declared.

"Yeah!" Christopher-John agreed. "Just let Papa get hold of 'em and he gonna turn 'em every which way but loose."

"Christopher-John, Man," Stacey said finally, "go get the cows and take them home."

"But we just brought them down here," Little Man protested.

"And we gotta pick the berries for dinner," said Christopher-John mournfully.

"No time for that now. Hurry up. And stay clear of them white men. Cassie, you come with me."

We ran, brown legs and feet flying high through the still forest.

By the time Stacey and I arrived at the house, Mr. Andersen's car was already parked in the dusty drive. Mr. Andersen himself was seated comfortably in Papa's rocker on the front porch. Big Ma was seated too, but Mama was standing.

Stacey and I eased quietly to the side of the porch, unnoticed.

"Sixty-five dollars. That's an awful lot of money in these hard times, Aunt Caroline," Mr. Andersen was saying to Big Ma.

I could see Mama's thin face harden.

"You know," Mr. Andersen said, rocking familiarly in Papa's chair, "that's more than David can send home in two months."

"We do quite well on what David sends home," Mama said coldly.

Mr. Andersen stopped rocking. "I suggest you encourage Aunt Caroline to sell them trees, Mary. You know, David might not always be able to work so good. He could possibly have . . . an accident."

Big Ma's soft brown eyes clouded over with fear as she looked first at Mr. Andersen, then at Mama. But Mama clenched her fists and said, "In Mississippi, black men do not have accidents."

"Hush, child, hush," Big Ma said hurriedly. "How many trees for the sixty-five dollars, Mr. Andersen?"

"Enough 'til I figure I got my sixty-five dollars' worth."

"And how many would that be?" Mama persisted.

Mr. Andersen looked haughtily at Mama. "I said I'd be the judge of that, Mary."

"I think not," Mama said.

Mr. Andersen stared at Mama. And Mama stared back at him. I knew Mr. Andersen didn't like that, but Mama did it anyway. Mr. Andersen soon grew uneasy under that piercing gaze, and when his eyes swiftly shifted from Mama to Big Ma, his face was beet-red.

"Caroline," he said, his voice low and menacing, "you're the head of this family and you've got a decision

to make. Now, I need them trees and I mean to have them. I've offered you a good price for them and I ain't gonna haggle over it. I know y'all can use the money. Doc Thomas tells me that Mary's not well." He hesitated a moment, then hissed venomously, "And if something should happen to David . . ."

"All right," Big Ma said, her voice trembling. "All right, Mr. Andersen."

"No, Big Ma!" I cried, leaping onto the porch. "You can't let him cut our trees!"

Mr. Andersen grasped the arms of the rocker, his knuckles chalk white. "You certainly ain't taught none of your younguns how to behave, Caroline," he said curtly.

"You children go on to the back," Mama said, shooing us away.

"No, Mama," Stacey said. "He's gonna cut them all down. Me and Cassie heard him say so in the woods."

"I won't let him cut them," I threatened. "I won't let him! The trees are my friends and ain't no mean ole white man gonna touch my trees ———"

Mama's hands went roughly around my body as she carried me off to my room.

"Now, hush," she said, her dark eyes flashing wildly. "I've told you how dangerous it is . . ." She broke off in midsentence. She stared at me a moment, then hugged me tightly and went back to the porch.

Stacey joined me a few seconds later, and we sat there in the heat of the quiet room, listening miserably as the first whack of an ax echoed against the trees.

That night I was awakened by soft sounds outside my window. I reached for Big Ma, but she wasn't there. Hurrying to the window, I saw Mama and Big Ma standing in the yard in their night clothes and Stacey, fully dressed, sitting atop Lady, our golden mare. By the time I got outside, Stacey was gone.

"Mama, where's Stacey?" I cried.

"Be quiet, Cassie. You'll wake Christopher-John and Little Man."

"But where's he going?"

"He's going to get Papa," Mama said. "Now be quiet."

"Go on Stacey, boy," I whispered. "Ride for me, too."

As the dust billowed after him, Mama said, "I should've gone myself. He's so young."

Big Ma put her arm around Mama. "Now, Mary, you know you couldn't 've gone. Mr. Andersen would miss

you if he come by and see you ain't here. You done right, now. Don't worry, that boy'll be just fine."

Three days passed, hot and windless.

Mama forbade any of us to go into the forest, so Christopher-John, Little Man and I spent the slow, restless days hovering as close to the dusty road as we dared, listening to the foreign sounds of steel against the trees and the thunderous roar of those ancient loved ones as they crashed upon the earth. Sometimes Mama would scold us and tell us to come back to the house, but even she could not ignore the continuous pounding of the axes against the trees. Or the sight of the loaded lumber wagons rolling out of the forest. In the middle of washing or ironing or hoeing, she would look up sorrowfully and listen, then turn toward the road, searching for some sign of Papa and Stacey.

On the fourth day, before the sun had risen bringing its cloak of miserable heat, I saw her walking alone toward the woods. I ran after her.

She did not send me back.

"Mama," I said, "how sick are you?"

Mama took my hand. "Remember when you had the flu and felt so sick?"

"Yes'm."

"And when I gave you some medicine, you got well soon afterward?"

"Yes'm."

"Well, that's how sick I am. As soon as I get my medicine, I'll be all well again. And that'll be soon now that Papa's coming home," she said, giving my hand a gentle little squeeze.

The quiet surrounded us as we entered the forest. Mama clicked on the flashlight and we walked silently along the cow path to the pond. There, just beyond the pond, pockets of open space loomed before us.

"Mama!"

"I know, baby, I know."

On the ground lay countless trees. Trees that had once been such strong, tall things. So strong that I could fling my arms partially around one of them and feel safe and secure. So tall and leafy green that their boughs had formed a forest temple.

And old.

So old that Indians had once built fires at their feet and had sung happy songs of happy days. So old, they had hidden fleeing black men in the night and listened to their

sad tales of a foreign land.

In the cold of winter when the ground lay frozen, they had sung their frosty ballads of years gone by. Or on a muggy, sweat-drenched day, their leaves had rippled softly, lazily, like restless green fingers strumming at a guitar, echoing their epic tales.

But now they would sing no more. They lay forever silent upon the ground.

Those trees that remained standing were like defeated warriors mourning their fallen dead. But soon they, too, would fall, for the white X's had been placed on nearly every one.

"Oh, dear, dear trees," I cried as the gray light of the rising sun fell in ghostly shadows over the land. The tears rolled hot down my cheeks. Mama held me close, and when I felt her body tremble, I knew she was crying too.

When our tears eased, we turned sadly toward the house. As we emerged from the forest, we could see two small figures waiting impatiently on the other side of the road. As soon as they spied us, they hurried across to meet us.

"Mama! You and Cassie was in the forest," Little Man accused. "Big Ma told us!"

"How was it?" asked Christopher-John, rubbing the sleep from his eyes. "Was it spooky?"

"Spooky and empty," I said listlessly.

"Mama, me and Christopher-John wanna see too," Little Man declared.

"No, baby," Mama said softly as we crossed the road. "The men'll be down there soon, and I don't want y'all underfoot."

"But, Mama ———" Little Man started to protest.

"When Papa comes home and the men are gone, then you can go. But until then, you stay out of there. You hear me, Little Man Logan?"

"Yes'm," Little Man reluctantly replied.

But the sun had been up only an hour when Little Man decided that he could not wait for Papa to return.

"Mama said we wasn't to go down there," Christopher-John warned.

"Cassie did," Little Man cried.

"But she was with Mama. Wasn't you, Cassie?"

"Well, I'm going too," said Little Man. "Everybody's always going someplace 'cepting me." And off he went.

Christopher-John and I ran after him. Down the narrow cow path and around the pond we chased. But neither of us was fast enough to overtake Little Man before he reached the lumbermen.

"Hey, you kids, get away from here," Mr. Andersen shouted when he saw us. "Now, y'all go on back home," he said, stopping in front of Little Man.

"We are home," I said. "You're the one who's on our land."

"Claude," Mr. Andersen said to one of the black lumbermen, "take these kids home." Then he pushed Little Man out of his way. Little Man pushed back. Mr. Andersen looked down, startled that a little black boy would do such a thing. He shoved Little Man a second time, and Little Man fell into the dirt.

Little Man looked down at his clothing covered with sawdust and dirt, and wailed, "You got my clothes dirty!"

I rushed toward Mr. Andersen, my fist in a mighty hammer, shouting, "You ain't got no right to push on Little Man. Why don't you push on somebody your own size—like me, you ole ——"

The man called Claude put his hand over my mouth and carried me away. Christopher-John trailed behind us, tugging on the man's shirt.

"Put her down. Hey, mister, put Cassie down."

The man carried me all the way to the pond. "Now," he said, "you and your brothers get on home before y'all get hurt. Go on, get!"

As the man walked away, I looked around. "Where's Little Man?"

Christopher-John looked around too.

"I don't know," he said. "I thought he was behind me."

Back we ran toward the lumbermen.

We found Little Man's clothing first, folded neatly by a tree. Then we saw Little Man, dragging a huge stick, and headed straight for Mr. Andersen.

"Little Man, come back here," I called.

But Little Man did not stop.

Mr. Andersen stood alone, barking orders, unaware of the oncoming Little Man.

"Little Man! Oh, Little Man, don't!"

It was too late.

Little Man swung the stick as hard as he could against Mr. Andersen's leg.

Mr. Andersen let out a howl and reached to where he thought Little Man's collar was. But, of course, Little Man had no collar.

"Run, Man!" Christopher-John and I shouted. "Run!"

"Why, you little . . ." Mr. Andersen cried, grabbing at Little Man. But Little Man was too quick for him. He slid right through Mr. Andersen's legs. Tom stood nearby, his face crinkling into an amused grin.

"Hey, y'all!" Mr. Andersen yelled to the lumbermen. "Claude! Get that kid!"

But sure-footed Little Man dodged the groping hands of the lumbermen as easily as if he were skirting mud puddles. Over tree stumps, around legs and through legs he dashed. But in the end, there were too many lumbermen for him, and he was handed over to Mr. Andersen.

For the second time, Christopher-John and I went to Little Man's rescue.

"Put him down!" we ordered, charging the lumbermen.

I was captured much too quickly, though not before I had landed several stinging blows. But Christopher-John, furious at seeing Little Man handled so roughly by Mr. Andersen, managed to elude the clutches of the lumbermen until he was fully upon Mr. Andersen. Then, with his mightiest thrust, he kicked Mr. Andersen solidly in the shins, not once, but twice, before the lumbermen pulled him away.

Mr. Andersen was fuming. He slowly took off his wide leather belt. Christopher-John, Little Man and I looked woefully at the belt, then at each other. Little Man and Christopher-John fought to escape, but I closed my eyes and awaited the whining of the heavy belt and its painful bite against my skin.

What was he waiting for? I started to open my eyes, but then the zinging whirl of the belt began and I tensed, awaiting its fearful sting. But just as the leather tip lashed into my leg, a deep familiar voice said, "Put the belt down, Andersen."

I opened my eyes.

"Papa!"

"Let the children go," Papa said. He was standing on a nearby ridge with a strange black box in his hands. Stacey was behind him holding the reins to Lady.

The chopping stopped as all eyes turned to Papa.

"They been right meddlesome," Mr. Andersen said. "They need teaching how to act."

"Any teaching, I'll do it. Now, let them go."

Mr. Andersen looked down at Little Man struggling to get away. Smiling broadly, he motioned our release. "Okay, David," he said.

As we ran up the ridge to Papa, Mr. Andersen said, "It's good to have you home, boy."

Papa said nothing until we were safely behind him. "Take them home, Stacey."

"But, Papa ——"

"Do like I say, son."

Stacey herded us away from the men. When we were far enough away so Papa couldn't see us, Stacey stopped and handed me Lady's reins.

"Y'all go on home now," he said. "I gotta go help Papa."

"Papa don't need no help," I said. "He told you to come with us."

"But you don't know what he's gonna do."

"What?" I asked.

"He's gonna blow up the forest if they don't get out of here. So go on home where y'all be safe."

"How's he gonna do that?" asked Little Man.

"We been setting sticks of dynamite since the middle of the night. We ain't even been up to the house cause Papa wanted the sticks planted and covered over before the men came. Now, Cassie, take them on back to the house.

Do like I tell you for once, will ya?" Then, without waiting for another word, he was gone.

"I wanna see," Little Man announced.

"I don't," protested Christopher-John.

"Come on," I said.

We tied the mare to a tree, then belly-crawled back to where we could see Papa and joined Stacey in the brush.

"Cassie, I told you . . ."

"What's Papa doing?"

The black box was now set upon a sawed-off tree stump, and Papa's hands were tightly grasping a T-shaped instrument which went into it.

"What's that thing?" asked Little Man.

"It's a plunger," Stacey whispered. "If Papa presses down on it, the whole forest will go pfffff!"

Our mouths went dry and our eyes went wide. Mr. Andersen's eyes were wide, too.

"You're bluffing, David," he said. "You ain't gonna push that plunger."

"One thing you can't seem to understand, Andersen," Papa said, "is that a black man's always gotta be ready to die. And it don't make me any difference if I die today or tomorrow. Just as long as I die right."

Mr. Andersen laughed uneasily. The lumbermen moved nervously away.

"I mean what I say," Papa said. "Ask anyone. I always mean what I say."

"He sure do, Mr. Andersen," Claude said, eyeing the black box. "He always do."

"Shut up!" Mr. Andersen snapped. "And the rest of y'all stay put." Then turning back to Papa, he smiled cunningly. "I'm sure you and me can work something out, David."

"Ain't nothing to be worked out," said Papa.

"Now, look here, David, your mama and me, we got us a contract . . ."

"There ain't no more contract," Papa replied coldly. "Now, either you get out or I blow it up. That's it."

"He means it, Mr. Andersen," another frightened lumberman ventured. "He's crazy and he sure 'nough means it."

"You know what could happen to you, boy?" Mr. Andersen exploded, his face beet-red again. "Threatening a white man like this?"

Papa said nothing. He just stood there, his hands firmly on the plunger, staring down at Mr. Andersen.

Mr. Andersen could not bear the stare. He turned away, cursing Papa. "You're a fool, David. A crazy fool." Then he looked around at the lumbermen. They shifted their eyes and would not look at him.

"Maybe we better leave, Mr. Andersen," Tom said quietly.

Mr. Andersen glanced at Tom, then turned back to Papa and said as lightly as he could, "All right, David, all right. It's your land. We'll just take the logs we got cut and get out." He motioned to the men. "Hey, let's get moving and get these logs out of here before this crazy fool gets us all killed."

"No," Papa said.

Mr. Andersen stopped, knowing that he could not have heard correctly. "What you say?"

"You ain't taking one more stick out of this forest."

"Now, look here ———"

"You heard me."

"But you can't sell all these logs, David," Mr. Andersen exclaimed incredulously.

Papa said nothing. Just cast that piercing look on Mr. Andersen.

"Look, I'm a fair man. I tell you what I'll do. I'll give you another thirty-five dollars. An even hundred dollars. Now, that's fair, ain't it?"

"I'll see them rot first."

"But ——"

"That's my last word," Papa said, tightening his grip on the plunger.

Mr. Andersen swallowed hard. "You won't always have that black box, David," he warned. "You know that, don't you?"

"That may be. But it won't matter none. Cause I'll always have my self-respect."

Mr. Andersen opened his mouth to speak, but no sound came. Tom and the lumbermen were quietly moving away, putting their gear in the empty lumber wagons. Mr. Andersen looked again at the black box. Finally, his face ashen, he too walked away.

Papa stood unmoving until the wagons and the men were gone. Then, when the sound of the last wagon rolling over the dry leaves could no longer be heard and a

hollow silence filled the air, he slowly removed his hands from the plunger and looked up at the remaining trees standing like lonely sentries in the morning.

"Dear, dear old trees," I heard him call softly, "will you ever sing again?"

I waited. But the trees gave no answer.

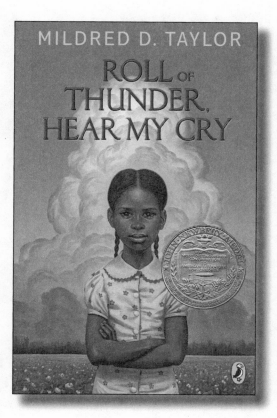

1

"Little Man, would you come on? You keep it up and you're gonna make us late."

My youngest brother paid no attention to me. Grasping more firmly his newspaper-wrapped notebook and his tin-can lunch of cornbread and oil sausages, he continued to concentrate on the dusty road. He lagged several feet behind my other brothers, Stacey and Christopher-John, and me, attempting to keep the rusty Mississippi dust from swelling with each step and drifting back upon his shiny black shoes and the cuffs of his corduroy pants by lifting each foot high before setting it gently down again. Always meticulously neat, six-year-old Little Man never allowed dirt or tears or stains to mar anything he owned. Today was no exception.

"You keep it up and make us late for school, Mama's gonna wear you out," I threatened, pulling with exasperation at the high collar of the Sunday dress Mama had made me wear for the first day of school—as if that event were something special. It seemed to me that showing up at school at all on a bright August-like October morning made for running the cool forest trails and wading barefoot in the forest pond was concession enough; Sunday clothing was asking too much. Christopher-John and Stacey were not too pleased about the clothing or school either. Only Little Man, just beginning his school career, found the prospects of both intriguing.

"Y'all go ahead and get dirty if y'all wanna," he replied without even looking up from his studied steps. "Me, I'm gonna stay clean."

"I betcha Mama's gonna 'clean' you, you keep it up," I grumbled.

"Ah, Cassie, leave him be," Stacey admonished, frowning and kicking testily at the road.

"I ain't said nothing but—"

Stacey cut me a wicked look and I grew silent. His disposition had been irritatingly sour lately. If I hadn't known the cause of it, I could have forgotten very easily that he was, at twelve, bigger than I, and that I had promised Mama to arrive at school looking clean and ladylike. "Shoot," I mumbled finally, unable to restrain myself from further comment, "it ain't my fault you gotta be in Mama's class this year."

Stacey's frown deepened and he jammed his fists into his pockets, but said nothing.

Christopher-John, walking between Stacey and me, glanced uneasily at both of us but did not interfere. A short, round boy of seven, he took little interest in troublesome things, preferring to remain on good terms with everyone. Yet he was always sensitive to others and now, shifting the handle of his lunch can from his right hand to his right wrist and his smudged notebook from his left hand to his left armpit, he stuffed his free hands into his pockets and attempted to make his face as moody as Stacey's and as cranky as mine. But after a few moments he seemed to forget that he was supposed to be grouchy and began whistling cheerfully. There was little that could make Christopher-John unhappy for very long, not even the thought of school.

I tugged again at my collar and dragged my feet in the dust, allowing it to sift back onto my socks and shoes like gritty red snow. I hated the dress. And the shoes. There was little I could do in a dress, and as for shoes, they imprisoned freedom-loving feet accustomed to the feel of the warm earth.

"Cassie, stop that," Stacey snapped as the dust billowed in swirling clouds around my feet. I looked up sharply, ready to protest. Christopher-John's whistling increased to a raucous, nervous shrill, and grudgingly I let the matter drop and trudged along in moody silence, my brothers growing as pensively quiet as I.

Before us the narrow, sun-splotched road wound like a lazy red serpent dividing the high forest bank of quiet, old trees on the left from the cotton field, forested by giant green and purple stalks, on the right. A barbed-wire fence ran the length of the deep field, stretching eastward for over a quarter of a mile until it met the sloping green pasture that signaled the end of our family's four hundred acres. An ancient oak tree on the slope, visible even now, was the official dividing mark between Logan land and the beginning of a dense forest. Beyond the protective fencing of the forest, vast farming fields, worked by a multitude of share-cropping families, covered two thirds of a ten-square-mile plantation. That was Harlan Granger land.

Once our land had been Granger land too, but the Grangers had sold it during Reconstruction to a Yankee for tax money. In 1887, when the land was up for sell again, Grandpa had bought two hundred acres of it, and in 1918, after the first two hundred acres had been paid off, he had bought another two hundred. It was good rich land, much of it still virgin forest, and there was no debt on half of it. But there was a mortgage on the two hundred acres bought in 1918 and there were taxes on the full four hundred, and for the past three years there had not been enough money from the cotton to pay both and live on too.

That was why Papa had gone to work on the railroad.

In 1930 the price of cotton dropped. And so, in the spring of 1931, Papa set out looking for work, going as far north as Memphis and as far south as the Delta country. He had gone west too, into Louisiana. It was there he found work laying track for the railroad. He worked the remainder of the year away from us, not returning until the deep winter when the ground was cold and barren. The following spring after the planting was finished, he did the same. Now it was 1933, and Papa was again in Louisiana laying track.

I asked him once why he had to go away, why the land was so important. He took my hand and said in his quiet way: "Look out there, Cassie girl. All that belongs to you. You ain't never had to live on nobody's place but your own and long as I live and the family survives, you'll never have to. That's important. You may not understand that now, but one day you will. Then you'll see."

I looked at Papa strangely when he said that, for I knew that all the land did not belong to me. Some of it belonged to Stacey, Christopher-John, and Little Man, not to mention the part that belonged to Big Ma, Mama, and Uncle Hammer, Papa's older brother who lived in Chicago. But Papa never divided the land in his mind; it was simply Logan land. For it he would work the long, hot summer pounding steel; Mama would teach and run the farm; Big Ma, in her sixties, would work like a woman of twenty in the fields and keep the house; and the boys and I would wear threadbare clothing washed to dishwater color; but always, the taxes and the mortgage would be paid. Papa said that one day I would understand.

I wondered.

When the fields ended and the Granger forest fanned both sides of the road with long overhanging branches, a tall, emaciated-looking boy popped suddenly from a forest trail and swung a thin arm around Stacey. It was T.J. Avery. His younger brother Claude emerged a moment later, smiling weakly as if it pained him to do so. Neither boy had on shoes, and their Sunday clothing, patched and worn, hung loosely upon their frail frames. The Avery family share-cropped on Granger land.

"Well," said T.J., jauntily swinging into step with Stacey, "here we go again startin' another school year."

"Yeah," sighed Stacey.

"Ah, man, don't look so down," T.J. said cheerfully. "Your mama's really one great teacher. I should know." He certainly should. He had failed Mama's class last year and was now returning for a second try.

"Shoot! You can say that," exclaimed Stacey. "You don't have to spend all day in a classroom with your mama."

"Look on the bright side," said T.J. "Jus' think of the advantage you've got. You'll be learnin' all sorts of stuff 'fore the rest of us. . . ." He smiled slyly. "Like what's on all them tests."

Stacey thrust T.J.'s arm from his shoulders. "If that's what you think, you don't know Mama."

"Ain't no need gettin' mad," T.J. replied undaunted.

"Jus' an idea." He was quiet for a moment, then announced, "I betcha I could give y'all an earful 'bout that burnin' last night."

"Burning? What burning?" asked Stacey.

"Man, don't y'all know nothin'? The Berrys' burnin'. I thought y'all's grandmother went over there last night to see 'bout 'em."

Of course we knew that Big Ma had gone to a sick house last night. She was good at medicines and people often called her instead of a doctor when they were sick. But we didn't know anything about any burnings, and I certainly didn't know anything about any Berrys either.

"What Berrys he talking 'bout, Stacey?" I asked. "I don't know no Berrys."

"They live way over on the other side of Smellings Creek. They come up to church sometimes," said Stacey absently. Then he turned back to T.J. "Mr. Lanier come by real late and got Big Ma. Said Mr. Berry was low sick and needed her to help nurse him, but he ain't said nothing 'bout no burning."

"He's low sick all right—'cause he got burnt near to death. Him and his two nephews. And you know who done it?"

"Who?" Stacey and I asked together.

"Well, since y'all don't seem to know nothin'," said T.J., in his usual sickening way of nursing a tidbit of information to death, "maybe I ought not tell y'all. It might hurt y'all's little ears."

"Ah, boy," I said, "don't start that mess again." I didn't like T.J. very much and his stalling around didn't help.

"Come on, T.J.," said Stacey, "out with it."

"Well . . ." T.J. murmured, then grew silent as if considering whether or not he should talk.

We reached the first of two crossroads and turned north; another mile and we would approach the second crossroads and turn east again.

Finally T.J. said, "Okay. See, them Berrys' burnin' wasn't no accident. Some white men took a match to 'em."

"Y-you mean just lit 'em up like a piece of wood?" stammered Christopher-John, his eyes growing big with disbelief.

"But why?" asked Stacey.

T.J. shrugged. "Don't know why. Jus' know they done it, that's all."

"How you know?" I questioned suspiciously.

He smiled smugly. "'Cause your mama come down on her way to school and talked to my mama 'bout it."

"She did?"

"Yeah, and you should've seen the way she look when she come outa that house."

"How'd she look?" inquired Little Man, interested enough to glance up from the road for the first time.

T.J. looked around grimly and whispered, "Like . . . death." He waited a moment for his words to be appropriately shocking, but the effect was spoiled by Little Man, who asked lightly, "What does death look like?"

T.J. turned in annoyance. "Don't he know nothin'?"

"Well, what does it look like?" Little Man demanded to know. He didn't like T.J. either.

"Like my grandfather looked jus' 'fore they buried him," T.J. described all-knowingly.

"Oh," replied Little Man, losing interest and concentrating on the road again.

"I tell ya, Stacey, man," said T.J. morosely, shaking his head, "sometimes I jus' don't know 'bout that family of yours."

Stacey pulled back, considering whether or not T.J.'s words were offensive, but T.J. immediately erased the question by continuing amiably. "Don't get me wrong, Stacey. They some real swell kids, but that Cassie 'bout got me whipped this mornin'."

"Good!" I said.

"Now how'd she do that?" Stacey laughed.

"You wouldn't be laughin' if it'd've happened to you. She up and told your mama 'bout me goin' up to that Wallace store dancin' room and Miz Logan told Mama." He eyed me disdainfully, then went on. "But don't worry, I got out of it though. When Mama asked me 'bout it, I jus' said ole Claude was always sneakin' up there to get some of that free candy Mr. Kaleb give out sometimes and I had to go and get him 'cause I knowed good and well she didn't want us up there. Boy, did he get it!" T.J. laughed. "Mama 'bout wore him out."

I stared at quiet Claude. "You let him do that?" I exclaimed. But Claude only smiled in that sickly way of his and I knew that he had. He was more afraid of T.J. than of his mother.

Again Little Man glanced up and I could see his dislike for T.J. growing. Friendly Christopher-John glared at T.J., and putting his short arm around Claude's shoulder said, "Come on, Claude, let's go on ahead." Then he and Claude hurried up the road, away from T.J.

Stacey, who generally overlooked T.J.'s underhanded stunts, shook his head. "That was dirty."

"Well, what'd ya expect me to do? I couldn't let her think I was goin' up there 'cause I like to, could I? She'd've killed me!"

"And good riddance," I thought, promising myself that if he ever pulled anything like that on me, I'd knock his block off.

THE LOGAN FAMILY'S STORY BEGAN IN

THE LAND

★ "Readers . . . will grab this and be astonished by its powerful story."　　　　　　　　　　　—*Booklist*, starred review

DAVID LOGAN ENDURES
GROWING TENSIONS IN

THE WELL

"Taylor has used her gift for storytelling and skillful char-
acterization to craft a brief but compelling novel about
prejudice and the saving power of human dignity."

—*School Library Journal*

JEREMY SIMMS IMPARTS HIS MEMORY
OF THE LOGANS IN

MISSISSIPPI BRIDGE

"Well written and thought provoking, this book will haunt readers and generate much discussion."

—*School Library Journal*

THE LOGAN CHILDREN SEE A
LIFELONG BOND TESTED IN

THE
FRIENDSHIP

"A powerful story . . . Readers will be haunted by its drama
and emotion long after they have closed the book."

—*Booklist*

THE LOGAN FAMILY REMAINS UNITED
THROUGH THE LOVE OF FAMILY
AND THEIR LAND IN

ROLL OF
THUNDER,
HEAR MY CRY

★ "The novel shows the rich inner rewards of black pride,
love, and independence."   —*Booklist,* starred review

THE LOGAN FAMILY PERSEVERES THROUGH
INCREASINGLY DIFFICULT TIMES IN

LET THE CIRCLE
BE UNBROKEN

"A profoundly affecting novel."   —*Publishers Weekly*

As World War II looms, Cassie fights
her own battle in

THE ROAD
TO
MEMPHIS

"An engrossing picture of fine young people endeavoring to find the right way in a world that persistently wrongs them." —*Kirkus Reviews*

A STORY OF PREJUDICE AND
FAMILY UNITY IS RECOUNTED IN

THE GOLD
CADILLAC

"A personal, poignant look at a black child's first experi-
ence with institutional racism."   —*The New York Times*

MILDRED D. TAYLOR

is the author of nine novels, including *The Road to Memphis*, *Let the Circle Be Unbroken*, *The Land*, and *Roll of Thunder, Hear My Cry*. Her books have won numerous awards, among them a Newbery Medal (for *Roll of Thunder, Hear My Cry*), four Coretta Scott King Awards, and a *Boston Globe–Horn Book* Award. Her book *The Land* was awarded an *L.A. Times* Book Prize and a PEN Award for Children's Literature. In 2003, Ms. Taylor was named the First Laureate of the NSK Neustadt Prize for Children's Literature. Ms. Taylor now devotes her time to her family, writing, and what she terms "the family ranch" in the foothills of the Rocky Mountains.